J
Har

Harris, Jack C

The frozen fiends

41922

DATE DUE

5/88

DEFENDERS OF THE EARTH

THE FROZEN FIENDS

DEFENDERS OF THE EARTH™

THE FROZEN FIENDS

by Jack C. Harris
illustrated by Gene Biggs

A GOLDEN BOOK • NEW YORK
Western Publishing Company, Inc., Racine, Wisconsin 53404

44922

Rockets screamed through the air as the great space
adventurer Flash Gordon piloted his flier low above a
top-secret U.S. atomic base.

"Your ray blasts are hitting Ming's Ice Robots," said
Mandrake the Magician, "but to no effect!"

"I hope the officials who called the Defenders of the Earth will not be disappointed," the Phantom whispered. "But I don't see how we can destroy Ming's robots."

"There must be some way," said Flash as he slowed down the superfast vehicle. "If we split up and use our individual powers, maybe we'll have success."

"Very well," the Phantom said. "Let me try."

The Phantom lowered himself silently to the frozen ground. A horde of Ice Robots advanced.

Quickly concentrating, the Phantom recited, "By jungle law, the Ghost Who Walks calls forth the power of ten tigers!" Suddenly the power was his.

The Ice Robots kept coming and the Phantom kept battling them. "I'm holding them off," he thought, "but even my strength cannot smash these creations!"

Nearby, Mandrake the Magician gestured magically and created a perfect illusion of a brick wall.

"The Ice Robots are harder than diamonds," thought the great master of magic. "Maybe I can fool them into halting their attack."

For an instant, the frozen slaves of Ming the Merciless hesitated before Mandrake's fake wall. But then they realized that the wall was not truly there, and pushed on.

"Mandrake," a voice called from above. It was Flash Gordon, speeding close to both the magician and the robots. "We must use a different plan. Climb aboard!"

"I see the wisdom of retreating for now," Mandrake admitted as he swung up into the flier.

"I can't understand it," said Flash. "How can Ming make ice that is harder than the hardest steel?"

"The Phantom's not having success either," Flash observed. He rocketed to pick up his masked partner.

As the Ghost Who Walks joined the other two members of the Defenders of the Earth, he heard Mandrake suggesting a new plan of action.

"We cannot damage these robots," Mandrake said. "But perhaps we can stop this attack by attacking them— indirectly." And he explained his plan.

Increasing the flier's speed, Flash circled the Ice Robots. At the same time, he cut a deep trench around them with the craft's ray cannons.

"Hurry," said the Phantom. "When they attacked us, they grouped together. Good. Now the entire horde of Ice Robots is surrounded by your trench."

"Shoot another blast under the section of ground they're on," Mandrake suggested.

Flash Gordon's thumbs drove down hard on his ray cannons' controls, and a superpowerful blast struck right underneath the Ice Robots.

"That'll take care of them," Flash said.

"You've done it, Flash," Mandrake said. "You've launched them right off the Earth!"

Meanwhile, Lothar, Mandrake's longtime friend and fellow Defender of the Earth, was just joining the younger Defenders inside their Monitor headquarters.

"Look, Lothar," called Rick Gordon, pointing to the computer screen of Dynak X. "Dad's blast not only got rid of the Ice Robots, but it freed the base."

"True," Lothar said, observing the thawed-out guards. "The base must have been covered with normal ice—not the kind the Robots are made of."

"Right, Dad," said L.J. "Our team stopped that attack, but they couldn't dent Ming's Ice Robots."

"Oh, no!" cried Kshin, Mandrake's apprentice. "Don't mention M–I–N–G in front of Zuffy. He goes wild!"

"Please keep him quiet," Rick pleaded. "Maybe Jedda can help. I have an idea. I'm programming Dynak X to search for all information about quick-freezing and temperature control. Maybe we can find something to break the 'iron ice' of those frozen fiends!"

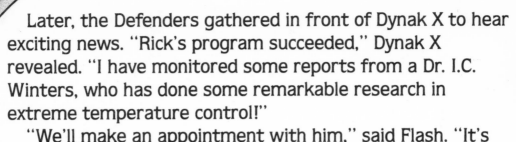

Later, the Defenders gathered in front of Dynak X to hear exciting news. "Rick's program succeeded," Dynak X revealed. "I have monitored some reports from a Dr. I.C. Winters, who has done some remarkable research in extreme temperature control!"

"We'll make an appointment with him," said Flash. "It's L.J.'s turn to come along on a mission with us."

"Rats, Zuffy!" Kshin complained. "You and I never get in on the *real* action."

At the very moment the Defenders were leaving, their greatest enemy was gloating. "Look at the fools," cried Ming the Merciless, his voice ringing through the halls of his Ice Station Earth. "They've tapped into the data *my* computer, Octon, 'planted' into the worldwide information network. They really believe that 'Dr. Winters' is going to help them. Ha! My trap is sprung!"

After contacting the famous scientist, the Defenders of the Earth met with Dr. I.C. Winters in his incredible frozen fortress.

"How do you do it, Doc?" asked L.J. "I mean, how does this chunk of ice stay solid in this summer heat?"

"It is but one use for my supercold blowers," explained Dr. Winters. "Now, how can I be of service to the great Defenders of the Earth?"

Back in the throne room of Ice Station Earth, Ming readied his evil plan. "I knew that the Defenders would discover that 'Dr. Winters' could help them against my Ice Robots. I planted all the clues and just waited for those pathetic earthlings to stumble across them.

"Now!" he yelled into a microphone. "Spring the trap now!"

Suddenly the lab of Dr. I.C. Winters seemed to come alive! From every shadowed nook and cranny, Ming's Ice Robots leapt forward. With their steel hardness and lightning-fast movements, they captured the Defenders in a matter of seconds.

"Look!" exclaimed L.J., watching wide-eyed as Dr. Winters peeled off his "skin." "Dr. Winters is really one of Ming's Men of Frost. We fell for a trap!"

Unknown to the Man of Frost called Dr. Winters, and unknown even to Ming the Merciless, the rest of the Defenders were already gathered at the base of the mountain.

"How did Flash Gordon know that this was all going to be some sort of trap?" asked Kshin.

"No time to explain now," Rick said as he handed a computer readout to his young friend. "Here's Dynak X's escape plan. Get it over to Jedda. Hurry!"

"Wow!" said Kshin, running as fast as he could around the base of the mountain. "I'm finally in on some action!"

As his feet dug into the ground he wished he could run faster. "Wait!" he thought. "I've got an idea!"

"Zuffy, come here!" Kshin called to his pet. Kshin passed the important message on to the team's mascot. "Go, Zuffy," he yelled. "It's up to you now!"

In seconds, Zuffy got the plan to Jedda, who was standing below the entrance to the icy mountain fortress. "It's a good plan," she said, and she went to work.

Using her special power to communicate with animals, the Phantom's daughter directed a hawk to secretly drop a tiny field mouse near the lock holding Lothar.

"Amazing," thought Lothar as the mouse crawled into the lock. "Jedda has made two natural enemies work together!"

There was a click and a scrape—and then the lock suddenly sprang open!

"The mouse was able to do what my great strength could not," Lothar observed. "My muscles and size were of no use on the delicate workings of the lock."

As he freed himself the hawk flew before him and gave him Dynak X's computer printout plan.

As soon as he knew what he had to do, Lothar was a blur of speed and strength. First he freed L.J.

"Move it, son," he said as he broke L.J.'s chains. "Here's what we have to do." Lothar explained the plan.

"Right, Dad," said L.J. as he rubbed his wrists. "It's a good thing my chains weren't as strong as yours."

With all his strength, Lothar hoisted his son to a catwalk high above them. Then he turned to face a group of attacking Ice Robots.

"Dynak X's plan is like a relay race," L.J. thought as he ran along the catwalk. "We each do our part to free another Defender. Jedda freed Dad, Dad freed me, and now it's up to me to free Mandrake."

L.J. followed a long icy corridor where he had seen some Ice Robots taking Mandrake. As he came upon them he yelled to Mandrake, "Go, free the Phantom!"

Then he used his skill in the martial arts to hold off the Ice Robots.

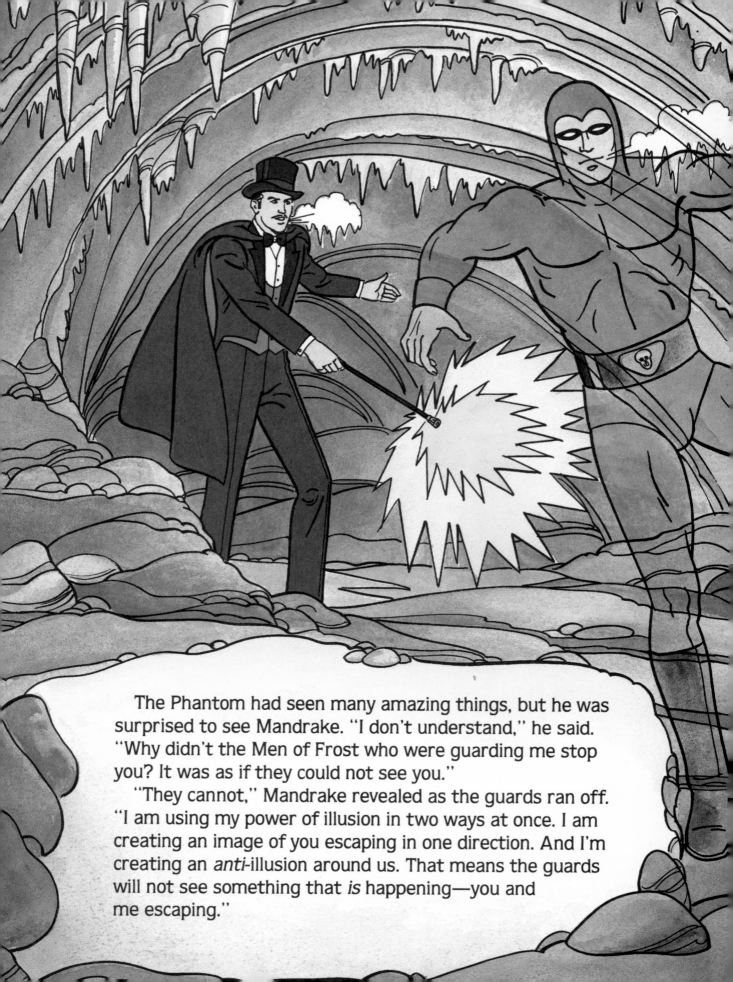

The Phantom had seen many amazing things, but he was surprised to see Mandrake. "I don't understand," he said. "Why didn't the Men of Frost who were guarding me stop you? It was as if they could not see you."

"They cannot," Mandrake revealed as the guards ran off. "I am using my power of illusion in two ways at once. I am creating an image of you escaping in one direction. And I'm creating an *anti*-illusion around us. That means the guards will not see something that *is* happening—you and me escaping."

Then Mandrake filled the Phantom in on the plan. "Brilliant," whispered the Phantom. "Now hold the illusion while I go free Flash Gordon. I saw where they were taking his iron-ice cage."

Racing to the cavern where Flash was held prisoner, the Phantom called on the power of ten tigers. He couldn't break Flash out of the cage because it was made of the same superice as the Ice Robots. Instead, he lifted the cage from its base.

"Excellent work, Phantom," said Flash as he ran out from under the cage. "Now, let's really put on the speed. I think I know how we can destroy the Ice Robots."

Flash raced across the lab and grabbed the superblower machine. "I saw how that phony scientist operated this device," he said. "Now watch."

As the other Defenders came running up to join him, Flash aimed the blower at the advancing Ice Robots.

"I get it," L.J. yelled in triumph. "The only thing hard enough to break an Ice Robot is *another* Ice Robot. And this blower is great for smashing them against each other!"

Soon all the Ice Robots had been smashed and the Men of Frost had fled. With the lab in shambles, the ice fortress began to melt. The Defenders headed for Rick's van.

"How did Rick, Jedda, and Kshin know we'd need them here?" asked L.J.

"Easy," explained Flash as they drove away from the melting mountain. "As soon as I saw that Dr. I.C. Winters had no icy breath in that cold place, I knew he wasn't human! I secretly radio-signaled Rick, and he had Dynak X devise a possible escape plan."

"What great teamwork," said Jedda. "It's something that Ming will never understand."

"You're right," Mandrake said. "As long as Ming works toward evil, his heart will be as cold as his Ice Robots."

As the Defenders of the Earth sped back to Central City, Ming watched them from Ice Station Earth. And no one was there to hear his scream of defeat.